Panda PaNTs

Panda PaNTs

BY JACQUELINE DAVIES

ILLUSTRATED BY

SYDNEY HANSON

ALFRED A. KNOPF 🐾 NEW YORK

"Pants have pockets."

"Not all pants."

"My pants would have pockets."

"Pants are warm."

"You have FUR. You don't need pants to keep warm."

"Pants would be warmer."

"Are you cold?"

"No. But I could be."

"At any moment."

"You will not be cold. At ANY moment. You are a panda. We do not wear pants."

"When have you ever seen pants on a panda?"

"Never. That's my point. Never on a panda."

"You will not be the first."

"I could be the first."

"But I COULD be."

"Everyone would admire my pants. They would LOVE them. My pants would impress."

"They really would."

"You are a PANDA! PANDAS DO NOT WEAR PANTS!"

"Hey. Pants!"

"Wait!"

"I've got
an idea."

"Impressive."

Splat!

"Why did you give away your pants?"

"I don't want pants."

"I want shoes."

For Julien and Santino—J.D.

For my dad—S.H.

THIS IS A BORZOI BOOK PUBLISHED BY ALFRED A. KNOPF

Text copyright © 2016 by Jacqueline Davies

Jacket art and interior illustrations copyright © 2016 by Sydney Hanson

All rights reserved. Published in the United States by Alfred A. Knopf, an imprint of Random House Children's Books,
a division of Penguin Random House LLC, New York.

Knopf, Borzoi Books, and the colophon are registered trademarks of Penguin Random House LLC.

Visit us on the Web! randomhousekids.com

Educators and librarians, for a variety of teaching tools, visit us at RHTeachersLibrarians.com

Library of Congress Cataloging-in-Publication Data

Davies, Jacqueline, author.

Panda pants / by Jacqueline Davies ; illustrated by Sydney Hanson. — First edition.

pages cm.

Summary: Panda wants to wear pants, but father Panda does not agree.

ISBN 978-0-553-53576-1 (trade) — ISBN 978-0-553-53577-8 (lib. bdg.) — ISBN 978-0-553-53578-5 (ebook)

1. Pandas—Juvenile fiction. 2. Pants—Juvenile fiction. [1. Pandas—Fiction. 2. Pants—Fiction.] I. Hanson, Sydney, illustrator. II. Title.

PZ7.D29392Pan 2016   [E]—dc23   2015007167

The illustrations in this book were created using mixed media.

MANUFACTURED IN CHINA

September 2016   10 9 8 7 6 5 4 3 2 1   First Edition